ANTHONY HOPE

The Prisoner of Zenda

Retold by Stephen Colbourn

MACMILLAN

BEGINNER LEVEL

Series Editor: John Milne

The Macmillan Guided Readers provide a choice of enjoyable reading material for learners of English. The series is published at five levels – Starter, Beginner, Elementary, Intermediate and Upper. At **Beginner Level**, the control of content and language has the following main features:

Information Control
The stories are written in a fluent and pleasing style with straightforward plots and a restricted number of main characters. The cultural background is made explicit through both words and illustrations. Information which is vital to the story is clearly presented and repeated where necessary.

Structure Control
Special care is taken with sentence length. Most sentences contain only one clause, though compound sentences are used occasionally with the clauses joined by the conjunctions 'and', 'but', and 'or'. The use of these compound sentences gives the text balance and rhythm. The use of Past Simple and Past Continuous Tenses is permitted since these are the basic tenses used in narration and students must become familiar with these as they continue to extend and develop their reading ability.

Vocabulary Control
At **Beginner Level** there is a controlled vocabulary of approximately 600 basic words, so that students with a basic knowledge of English will be able to read with understanding and enjoyment. Help is also given in the form of vivid illustrations which are closely related to the text.

For further information on the full selection of Readers at all five levels in the series, please refer to the Macmillan Readers catalogue.

Contents

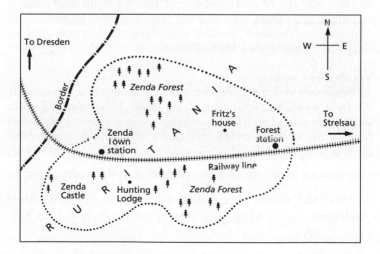

A Note About the Author

Anthony Hope (Sir Anthony Hope Hawkins) was born in London on 9th February 1863. His father was the headmaster of a school. From 1876 to 1881, Anthony Hope was a student at Marlborough – a famous school for boys. He was a good student and a good athlete. From 1881 to 1883, Anthony Hope studied at Balliol College in Oxford University. In 1887, he became a lawyer in London.

After 1895, Anthony Hope did not work as a lawyer. He became an author. He wrote many plays and stories. His most famous stories are: *The Man of the Mark* (1890), *The Prisoner of Zenda* (1894) and *Rupert of Hentzau* (1898).

Many plays and films were made of Anthony Hope's stories. Films were made of *The Prisoner of Zenda* in 1913, 1922, 1937, 1952 and 1979.

In 1903, Anthony Hope married an American – Betty Somerville. They had three children – two sons and a daughter. In the First World War (1914-1918), Anthony Hope worked for the British Government. In 1918, Hope was given a knighthood. He was called Sir Anthony Hope Hawkins. He died on 8th July 1933. He was 70 years old.

A Note About This Story

Time: 1893. **Place:** The country of Ruritania, somewhere in Central Europe.

This is a romantic story. And it is an adventure story. The author wrote many stories about beautiful women and handsome men. In these stories, men wore fine uniforms. They fought with swords and they rode fast horses. Some of these people lived in palaces and castles. Castles were strong buildings made of stone.

This story happens in Ruritania. Ruritania is not a real country. There has never been a country called Ruritania. There is not a town called Zenda.

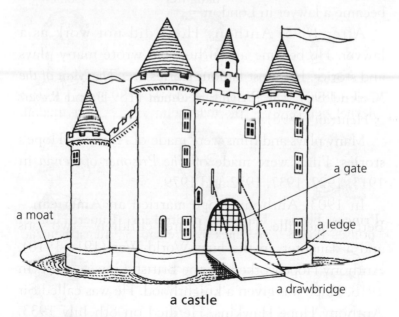

a gate

a moat

a ledge

a drawbridge

a castle

Note: The letters 'ph' in Elphberg = 'f'.

The People in This Story

**Rudolf
Rassendyll**
'ruːdɒlf 'ræsəndɪl

**Rose
Rassendyll**
rəʊz 'ræsəndɪl

George
dʒɔːdʒ

**Antoinette
de Mauban**
ɒntwʌneɪt də 'məʊbɒ

The innkeeper

**The innkeeper's
daughter**

Johann
'jəʊhæn

Colonel Sapt
'kɜːnəl zæpt

Fritz Tarlenheim
frɪts 'tɑːlənheɪm

Prince Rudolf
prɪns 'ruːdɒlf

Princess Flavia
prɪnses 'flɑːvɪə

The Duke of Strelsau
ðə djuːk əv 'strelzaʊ

Rupert Hentzau
'ruːpət 'hentzaʊ

Detchard
'detʃɑːd

De Gautet
də 'gəʊteɪ

Bersonin
'beərsəʊnæ

6

1

The Rassendyll Family

My name is Rudolf Rassendyll. I am tall and strong. I have red hair and a red beard. And I have a long, thin nose.

I am an English gentleman. I do not have a job. But every year, I travel in Europe. I can speak French and German. I speak those languages very well. I can speak Italian and Spanish too.

I read many books and I am interested in many things. I can ride a horse. I can fight with a sword and I can hunt with a gun.

The Rassendyll family is a rich English family. But there is a scandal about the Rassendyll family.

My great-grandfather was called Rudolf too. But he was not an Englishman. He was Rudolf Elphberg and he had royal blood.

Rudolf Elphberg visited London in 1733. He was a young, very good-looking man. He was tall and strong, and he had red hair. And he was a prince! His father was King of Ruritania.

My great-grandmother was a young lady in 1733. She was not married. She lived at the palace of the King of England. One day, Rudolf Elphberg visited the King of England. My great-grandmother saw the young, red-haired prince. She fell in love with him. And he fell in love with her.

A few months later, the King of Ruritania died. Rudolf Elphberg went back to Ruritania. He became the king of his country. He became King Rudolf the Third. He married a German princess and he never met my great-grandmother again.

Soon after that, my great-grandmother got married. Her husband was a rich English gentleman. His name was Rassendyll. He was a short man with black hair. The next year, my great-grandmother had a baby. The baby boy's hair was red.

Mr Rassendyll was not the boy's father. The boy's father was Rudolf Elphberg. This was a scandal in England in 1734. And this is the scandal about the Rassendyll family.

2

A New King for Ruritania

In 1893, I was twenty-nine years old. In the summer, I was staying at my brother's house in London. My brother is a diplomat. He works for the government.

One morning, I was talking to my brother's wife. Her name is Rose. My brother was not at home that morning. My sister-in-law and I were eating breakfast.

'Rudolf,' Rose said. 'You are nearly thirty years old. You must get a job.'

'I don't want a job, Rose,' I said.

'We will find you a job in an embassy,' my sister-in-law said. 'You must work in an embassy in Europe. You must become a diplomat. You enjoy your visits to Europe. You speak French and German well.'

'Yes, I speak those languages well,' I said. 'I studied at a school in Germany, Rose.'

'And your great-grandfather was German,' Rose said.

'No, he wasn't German,' I said. 'He was Ruritanian. His name was Rudolf Elphberg. He became King of Ruritania.'

'Yes! The Rassendyll family has royal blood,' said my sister-in-law.

'The Rassendylls' royal blood is our family's secret,' I said. 'Our royal blood is a scandal, Rose!'

'You must not think about that old scandal, Rudolf,' said Rose.

'I'm going out,' I said. 'I will see you this evening.'

Later that morning, I saw an article in the *Times* newspaper.

A NEW KING FOR RURITANIA

23rd July, 1893

There is news from Strelsau, the capital of Ruritania. King Rudolf IV of Ruritania is dead. The King's younger son, Prince Rudolf, will become King Rudolf V. The coronation will happen in three weeks. The Bishop of Strelsau will put the crown of Ruritania on the prince's head. The coronation will happen in Strelsau Cathedral.

I read the article three times. I thought about my sister-in-law's words. I did not want a job. But I wanted a holiday.

'I will visit Strelsau,' I said to myself. 'I will see the coronation of Prince Rudolf.'

I did not tell my sister-in-law about my plan. But that evening, I spoke to her again.

'I *will* go to Europe, Rose,' I said. 'I will go to Germany. I will travel to Dresden. I will visit some friends there. And I will walk in the mountains.'

'You must write a book, Rudolf,' said my sister-in-law. 'Write a book about your visit to Germany. After that, we will find you a job in an embassy.'

'Yes, Rose,' I said. 'I will leave London tomorrow. I will go to Paris. Then I will go to Dresden. I will write to you from Dresden. And I will write a book.'

———

Two days later, I arrived in Paris. I was going to stay with two of my friends, George and Bertram.

George knew many people in London, Paris, Brussels and Berlin. He knew many people in Rome, Madrid – and Strelsau! George wrote letters to his friends. And George's friends wrote letters to him. His friends told him the news from every capital city in Europe.

George met me at the railway station. He took me to his house. Bertram was not there.

'I'm going to tell you a secret,' he told me.

'What is your secret, George?' I asked.

'Bertram is in love!' George replied. 'He loves a French lady. Her name is Antoinette de Mauban,' said George. 'Her husband is dead – she is a widow. She is very beautiful.'

'And does this beautiful lady love Bertram?' I asked.

'No, Madame de Mauban doesn't love Bertram,' said George. 'She loves the Duke of Strelsau.'

'The Duke of Strelsau? Is he the older brother of Prince Rudolf of Ruritania?' I asked.

'He is the half-brother of Prince Rudolf,' George answered. 'The two men had different mothers.'

'Prince Rudolf will become the King of Ruritania next week,' I said. 'The bishop will put the crown on his head in Strelsau Cathedral. The prince will become King Rudolf the Fifth. I read about it in the *Times*.'

'But I hear news from diplomats,' George said. 'Last week, I heard some news from a German diplomat. I met him at Madame de Mauban's house, outside Paris. He told me a strange story. He said, "The Duke of Strelsau will be the new king of Ruritania. He will be King Michael the First." That is interesting news!'

'But it is not true,' I said. 'Prince Rudolf will be the new king.'

'The Duke of Strelsau is older than Prince Rudolf,'

said George. 'And the Duke wants to be the King of Ruritania. But Rudolf the Fourth did not marry the Duke's mother. It was a scandal!'

'I know about scandals!' I said. 'What will happen to Prince Rudolf? Does he want to be king?'

'Nobody knows about that,' said George. 'Prince Rudolf did not like his father. The Prince has lived in France for many years. But now he has returned to Ruritania. And he is going to marry his cousin, Princess Flavia.'

'But the Duke of Strelsau wants to marry Princess Flavia too,' said George. 'And Madame de Mauban wants to marry the Duke of Strelsau. The German diplomat told me this story.'

'I don't believe that German diplomat's story,' I said. 'But I'm going to visit Ruritania soon. I will leave Paris in two weeks. I'll write to you from Ruritania, George. And I'll tell you the news from Strelsau!'

Then we left the station.

3

Zenda

Two weeks later, George took me back to the railway station. It was a fine morning. I bought a ticket for Dresden. Then George and I walked towards my train.

Suddenly George stopped.

'Rudolf! There's Bertram's friend!' he said.

'Who is Bertram's friend?' I asked.

George pointed to a tall, dark woman. The woman was wearing beautiful, expensive clothes.

'That's Antoinette de Mauban,' said George. 'She's getting onto the train to Dresden.'

I got into the train. It was going to leave in a few minutes.

'Goodbye, George,' I said. 'I'll write to you.'

Soon I was travelling across France.

The journey to Dresden was long and tiring. Sometimes I looked out of the window. Sometimes I slept. I did not see Madame de Mauban on the train. But the next day, I saw her at the railway station in Dresden. She was a beautiful woman.

———

I stayed in Dresden for a day and a night. I visited some friends. I wrote to my sister-in-law.

The next day was Monday. In the afternoon, I went to Dresden railway station and I bought a ticket to Strelsau. Madame de Mauban was at the station too.

'Is she going to Ruritania?' I asked myself. 'Is she going to see the coronation?'

I found the train to Strelsau quickly and I got into it. Soon the train started its journey.

After fifteen minutes, the train stopped. It stopped at the border between Germany and Ruritania. Some Ruritanian border officials got into the train. They looked at everybody's travel documents.

One of the officials looked at my documents. Then he looked at my face carefully. Was he surprised about something? After a few moments, he gave me back my travel documents.

'I want to stay in Strelsau,' I told him. 'Where shall I stay? Is there a good hotel in the city?'

'The new king's coronation is going to happen on Wednesday, sir,' said the man. 'There are many visitors in Strelsau. All the hotels are full.'

'Where *shall* I stay?' I asked the official. 'Where can I get a hotel room in Ruritania?'

'There is a small town, eighteen kilometres from here,' the official told me. 'The town is called Zenda. There is a good inn in the town. You will get a room at that inn. This train stops at Zenda. You must get off the train there.'

'Is the journey from Zenda to Strelsau a long journey?' I asked.

'No, sir,' the man said. 'Strelsau is ninety kilometres from Zenda. Do you want to see the coronation?'

'Yes, I want to see King Rudolf.'

'You must stay at the inn in Zenda, sir,' said the man. 'And you must go to Strelsau by train on Wednesday. It is a two-hour journey.'

I thanked the official and he walked away.

———

Thirty minutes later, the train arrived at Zenda station. I got off the train. Madame de Mauban did not get off.

'The lady is travelling to Strelsau.' I thought.

I stood outside the railway station and I looked at the small town. Around Zenda there was a great forest. And there was a big hill behind the town. The forest covered the hill. But on the top of the hill, there was an old castle.

I picked up my cases and I walked into the town. Soon, I found the inn. I went inside and I spoke to the innkeeper. I asked him for a room.

The innkeeper was a kind, polite man. He took me up some stairs to a large bedroom. It was a comfortable room.

'Here is your room, sir,' the innkeeper said. 'Come downstairs in half an hour. My daughter will bring you a hot meal.'

Half an hour later, I was sitting in a dining-room. The innkeeper's daughter brought me a meal. The food was good.

The innkeeper's daughter was a pretty girl and she was friendly and polite. She was about seventeen years old.

'Who lives in the castle on the hill?' I asked her.

'That's Black Michael's castle,' the girl answered.

Suddenly, I heard a man's voice.

'The owner of the castle is Duke Michael of Strelsau,' the man said loudly. 'And who are you, sir?'

I looked round. A big man was standing near the door of the room. The innkeeper's daughter turned towards him.

'Hello, Johann,' she said. 'This gentleman is visiting Zenda. He is a traveller from England.'

'You must tell strangers the Duke's correct name,' Johann said to her. 'He is Duke Michael of Strelsau. You must not call him Black Michael!'

Then Johann walked towards us. He looked at me

carefully. He looked at my face and he looked at my hair. I remembered the border official on the train. He had looked at me carefully too. Had he been surprised about something? Was Johann surprised about something? Yes, Johann was surprised!

'Do you know Prince Rudolf, sir?' he asked politely.

'No,' I replied. 'I have never seen the Prince. But my name is Rudolf too. My name is Rudolf Rassendyll.'

'You have red hair,' said Johann. 'Prince Rudolf has red hair too.'

'The Prince will become King Rudolf soon,' said the innkeeper's daughter. 'His coronation will happen on Wednesday.'

'I want to see the coronation,' I said. 'But all the hotels in Strelsau are full.'

'I am going to see the coronation,' Johann said to me. 'I have a sister in Strelsau. I'm going to stay with her.'

Then he spoke to the innkeeper's daughter.

'I must go back to the castle now, my dear,' he said. 'I will go to Strelsau tomorrow evening. But I will come here tomorrow morning. I will see you then. Goodnight!'

Then he turned to me.

'Goodnight, sir,' he said. 'Sleep well!'

He left the room quickly.

Later, the innkeeper talked to me. He told me about Johann.

'Johann is one of Duke Michael's servants,' he said. 'He works at Zenda Castle. Duke Michael often stays at the castle. And Johann often comes here to the inn. He wants to marry my daughter.'

4

In the Forest

The next morning, Johann came to the inn again. There was a letter in his hand. He spoke to me. He was polite and friendly.

'I cannot go to Strelsau today,' he said. 'I cannot leave the castle. You want to see the coronation tomorrow, sir. You can travel to Strelsau today. Give this letter to my sister. Stay at her house tonight, and go to the cathedral tomorrow. My sister's house is very comfortable. You will enjoy your visit to the capital. And you will enjoy the coronation.'

'Thank you, Johann,' I said. 'You are very kind. I will take the letter to your sister. And I will stay at her house. This morning, I will send my cases to Strelsau by train. Then I will walk in Zenda Forest for an hour or two. Is there a railway station at the other side of the forest?'

'Yes, sir,' Johann answered. 'It is eight kilometres from here. The train to Strelsau stops there.'

'Good!' I said. 'I want to look at the castle. Later, I will walk to the forest station. Then I will take the afternoon train to Strelsau. I will get on the train at the forest station.'

Johann gave me the letter for his sister.

'Bring your cases down from your room, sir,' he said. 'I will carry them to Zenda station now.'

Soon, Johann left the inn. He took my cases to the railway station. ——

Later that morning, I left the inn. I walked towards the hill behind the town. I wanted to look at Zenda Castle. Then I was going to walk in Zenda Forest.

The hill behind the town of Zenda was very steep. I walked up it very slowly. I walked towards Black Michael's castle. At last, I arrived at the top of the hill.

There was a moat around Zenda Castle. The moat was deep and it was full of water. I walked around the edge of the moat.

I saw only one entrance to the castle. The entrance was a huge, strong gate in the castle wall. There was a drawbridge across the moat. The road from the town ended at the drawbridge.

'Duke Michael is safe in his castle,' I thought. 'At night, the servants pull up the drawbridge. Then nobody can cross the moat. Nobody can get into the castle. And nobody can leave it!'

For two hours, I walked in Zenda Forest. The forest was very thick. The trees grew close together. It was a warm day. The birds were singing. The sun was shining through the pine trees. The trees had a sweet smell.

At about three o'clock, I sat down. I sat against a tree. 'I will close my eyes for a minute,' I thought.

But I fell asleep. I slept for a long time.

I woke suddenly and I opened my eyes. Two men were looking at me. Both men were holding hunting-guns.

One of the men was about sixty years old. He was strong and heavy. He had short white hair and a white moustache. The other man was young and handsome. He had dark hair. The two men were talking about me.

I stood up.

'Good afternoon, sir!' said the old man. 'What is your name?'

'My name is Rudolf Rassendyll,' I replied. 'I am a visitor from England. And what is *your* name, sir?'

'I am Colonel Sapt,' said the old man. 'And this is Fritz Tarlenheim.'

Then we heard another voice.

'Fritz! Sapt!' a man shouted. 'Where are you?'

A man came towards us through the trees. He was carrying a hunting-gun too. Suddenly, he stopped and he looked at me. For half a minute, we looked at each other.

The man had red hair. I have red hair. The man was tall. I am tall. The man had a long, thin nose. I have a long, thin nose. But I have a beard and this man did not have a beard.

Colonel Sapt spoke to the red-haired man.

'Sir,' he said. 'This is Mr Rudolf Rassendyll from England.'

'Rudolf! He has my name,' said the red-haired man. 'And he has a long, thin nose and red hair. Do we have the same great-grandfather?' The man laughed.

'Prince Rudolf Elphberg was my great-grandfather, sir,' I said.

'Mr Rassendyll, you are my cousin!' the red-haired man said. I am Prince Rudolf of Ruritania.'

Was I surprised? No, I was not surprised. The border official on the train had looked at me carefully. *He* had been surprised. Johann had looked at me carefully too. At last, I understood!

'We will talk together,' said the Prince. 'Come to my hunting-lodge. Eat dinner with me tonight!'

'Sir, we must leave the lodge early tomorrow,' said Fritz Tarlenheim. 'We must go the railway station at eight o'clock in the morning.'

'Yes, I will wake early,' said the Prince. 'But I want to talk to my cousin tonight.'

We started to walk through the forest. Prince Rudolf asked me many questions about my family.

After half an hour, we came to the Prince's hunting-lodge. The hunting-lodge was a wooden building in the forest. We went into the lodge. The Prince spoke to a servant.

'This gentleman will eat with us,' the Prince said. 'Bring our dinner in ten minutes, please.'

Prince Rudolf, Colonel Sapt and Fritz Tarlenheim sat down at a table. I sat down with them.

The servant brought us food and wine.

'We must leave for Strelsau early tomorrow, sir,' Colonel Sapt said to the Prince. 'Don't drink a lot of wine.'

'I shall drink with my cousin,' said the Prince. He picked up a large black bottle.

'Here is a bottle of good wine,' he said. 'This is a gift from my half-brother. Let us drink Black Michael's wine!'

'You call him Black Michael, sir?' I asked.

'Everybody calls him Black Michael,' said the Prince.

He opened the bottle. Colonel Sapt and Fritz Tarlenheim drank a little of the wine. I drank one glass of it. The Prince drank the rest of the wine quickly.

'Long live Black Michael!' said Prince Rudolf. 'Long live the Duke of Strelsau!'

5

Black Michael

Somebody threw some cold water over my head! I was lying on the floor. Some more cold water hit my face.

I stood up very quickly. Colonel Sapt and Fritz Tarlenheim were standing in front of me. Colonel Sapt was holding a bucket.

'Stop!' I shouted. 'Why did you do that?'

'I'm sorry, Mr Rassendyll,' the colonel said. 'I could not wake you. There is a problem, sir. Look at the Prince.'

Prince Rudolf was lying on the floor. His face was very pale. His mouth was open and his eyes were closed.

'Is the Prince dead?' I asked.

'No, he isn't dead,' said Colonel Sapt. 'He is sleeping. But we cannot wake him. Black Michael put a drug in that wine. Prince Rudolf will sleep for many hours. We only drank a little of the wine, but we have slept all night.'

'What is the time?' I asked.

'It's six o'clock on Wednesday morning,' said Fritz Tarlenheim. 'It is the Prince's coronation day.'

'We must be at the railway station at eight o'clock,' said Colonel Sapt. 'And you must be there with us!'

'Why?' I asked. 'What is happening?'

'We are going to take you to Strelsau,' said the

colonel. 'Today you will be King Rudolf the Fifth!'

'No,' I said. 'No! What are you saying?'

'The Prince cannot go to his coronation,' said Fritz.

'But Ruritania must have a king today!' the colonel said. 'This is a very serious problem, Mr Rassendyll. Fritz and I have talked together. We have a plan.'

'Prince Rudolf has lived in France for many years,' said Fritz. 'The people of Strelsau have not often seen him. The Prince is tall and he has red hair. You are tall and you have red hair, Mr Rassendyll. The Prince has a long, thin nose. You have a long, thin nose too.'

'The Prince doesn't have a beard,' said Sapt. 'We will shave off your beard. Then you must be our king for one day. This afternoon, we will take you to Strelsau Cathedral. The Bishop of Strelsau will put the crown on your head. But tonight, you must leave Ruritania. And you must never come back!'

'No!' I said again. 'This is not possible!'

'Please help us, Mr Rassendyll,' said Colonel Sapt. 'Help us! Save your cousin's life!'

'My cousin's life? I do not understand,' I said.

'Black Michael wants to be the King of Ruritania,' said Fritz. 'He wants to kill Prince Rudolf. And Black Michael wants to kill the Prince's friends. He wants to kill all of us!'

'Prince Rudolf cannot go to Strelsau today,' said Sapt. 'The people of Strelsau will be waiting in the cathedral. Black Michael will say, "Prince Rudolf has died." The bishop will put the crown on Michael's head. He will be the King of Ruritania.'

'But Black Michael will be bad for our country,' the colonel said. 'He must not be the King of Ruritania! Prince Rudolf must be our King! Please, Mr Rassendyll, help us. Please, help Ruritania!'

I looked at Colonel Sapt and Fritz Tarlenheim. They were very worried. They were good men. I liked them. I did not like their plan, but I wanted to help my cousin.

'I will help you,' I said. But I was not happy.

The servant went to another room and he returned with a white-and-gold uniform.

'This is the King's coronation uniform,' Fritz said.

'Do not be afraid, Mr Rassendyll,' said the colonel. 'We will help you. I will stand by your side in the cathedral. Now, we will shave off your beard.'

The servant brought some soap and a razor. Colonel Sapt shaved off my beard. The colonel worked and Fritz talked to me.

Fritz told me about Prince Rudolf's life. Then he told me about the city of Strelsau. He told me about the great cathedral and about the royal palace.

I put on the white-and-gold coronation uniform. The uniform fitted me well. I looked in a mirror. I did not see myself. I saw Prince Rudolf!

'Now you are Prince Rudolf,' said the colonel. 'We will put the real prince in his bed. He will sleep here in the hunting-lodge all day. And tonight, we will come and wake him. Now we must go to the station.'

We rode on horses through the forest. Soon, we came to a small railway station. A train was waiting for us. And many soldiers were waiting for us. They were wearing red uniforms. They raised their hands and they saluted me.

'These soldiers are the Royal Guards,' said Sapt.

We all got into a train. Soon, we started our journey to Strelsau. Colonel Sapt talked to me on the journey.

'Today, you will be the King,' he said. 'This is your coronation day. You will go to the cathedral. The Bishop of Strelsau will put the crown on your head. After the coronation, you will go to the royal palace. Then you will rest. Nobody will speak to you.'

'Tonight, we will ride back to the hunting-lodge,' said the colonel. 'The real King Rudolf will be awake. We will take him back to Strelsau. You will sleep at the hunting-lodge. And tomorrow morning, you will leave the country. You will never return to Ruritania.'

———

The train arrived in Strelsau. Thousands of people were waiting for me. A band was playing loud music. There were many soldiers in black-and-gold uniforms. I got off the train. The people smiled and cheered. The soldiers saluted me.

A large man with a black beard walked towards me. His face was pale and his dark eyes were cruel. It was Black Michael! He saluted me. He spoke a few words. But he was very surprised. And he was very angry!

6

Strelsau

Black Michael rode to the Cathedral of Strelsau on a big white horse. The Royal Guards – the soldiers in red uniforms – walked behind him. I followed them on a beautiful black horse. Colonel Sapt rode on my right. Fritz Tarlenheim rode on my left. The soldiers in black-and-gold uniforms rode on horses behind us.

The cathedral was full of people. The choir sang. After that, the Bishop of Strelsau spoke the words of the coronation. Then he put a heavy gold crown on my head – the crown of Ruritania! The choir sang again. The people shouted, 'Long live King Rudolf!'

After the coronation, I went to the royal palace. I went there in a carriage. Princess Flavia sat beside me.

'The Princess has not seen Prince Rudolf for many months,' I thought. 'Fritz told me that. But she is Rudolf's cousin. I must be careful!'

I looked at Princess Flavia. She was a beautiful young woman. She had wonderful red hair. She was an Elphberg too!

'You are different person today, cousin,' she said.

'Yes, I am a different person,' I replied. 'I am the King of Ruritania!'

'Yes, you are the King,' Princess Flavia said quietly.

'I am very happy,' I said.

'Your half-brother is not happy,' said the Princess. 'Be careful, Rudolf. Duke Michael is a very dangerous man!'

'I know that, cousin,' I said. 'I will be careful.'

'And the Duke has six very dangerous friends,' said the Princess. 'You know about the Six, Rudolf.'

'Yes, I know about the Six,' I said.

I knew nothing about the Six. But I knew something. I liked Princess Flavia very much!

A few minutes later, Colonel Sapt met me at the royal palace. He took me to the king's bedroom.

'The King is tired,' Sapt told the palace officials. 'He must rest now. I will stay with him.'

At last, Sapt and I were alone. The colonel gave me a dark cloak, a large hat and a long scarf.

'Put these on,' said Colonel Sapt. 'We must ride back to the hunting-lodge. You are an English gentleman again, Mr Rassendyll. You are not the King now. The real king must come to Strelsau tonight. But first, King Rudolf must thank you for your help. We must leave soon.'

It was dark in the streets of Strelsau. Near the palace, Fritz was waiting with two horses. Colonel Sapt and I got onto the horses. We rode through the streets of the city. Then we left Strelsau and we rode towards the Forest of Zenda.

'Colonel, who are the Six?' I asked.

'They are the friends of Black Michael,' answered Colonel Sapt. 'They are bad men. They are criminals! Three of the men are Ruritanians. Three of them are foreigners. All of them are bad men!'

We arrived at the hunting-lodge after midnight. No lights were shining in the windows of the building.

'The King has not woken,' said the colonel. He opened the door of the lodge.

'Your Majesty!' he called, 'Your Majesty, wake up!'

Nobody answered.

Colonel Sapt found a lamp. He lit it. We looked around. The hunting-lodge was empty!

We went into the dining-room. We were both very worried.

'Look, colonel!' I said. I pointed to the floor near a cupboard. 'There is some blood on the floor here!'

The colonel opened the door of the cupboard. Inside the cupboard we found the servant. There was a knife in his body. He was dead!

'The Six killed this man,' said Colonel Sapt. 'They have taken the King away.'

'What shall we do?' I asked.

'We shall return to Strelsau immediately,' said Sapt. 'You are the King of Ruritania again, Mr Rassendyll!'

7
The Six

Colonel Sapt and I rode back to Strelsau. Sapt told me
about the government of Ruritania. We made some
new plans.

'Mr Rassendyll, you must meet some government
ministers tomorrow,' the colonel said. 'And you must
meet some diplomats from other countries.'

'What shall I say to them?' I asked him.

'Don't say anything,' Sapt said. 'And don't worry.
I'll help you. But you must speak to Princess Flavia.
You must speak about the plans for her marriage. Black
Michael wants to marry her. That will be bad for
Ruritania. The Princess must not marry Black Michael.
She must marry the King.'

I did not answer. I liked the Princess very much. But
I was not the real king.

———

Colonel Sapt and I arrived in Strelsau. It was eight
o'clock in the morning. We left our horses half a mile
from the royal palace.

Ten minutes later, we walked into the palace. My
hat and my scarf covered my face. But the soldiers
knew the colonel and nobody stopped us. We went to
the king's bedroom.

Fritz Tarlenheim was waiting for us.

'Your Majesty,' Fritz said to me. 'You are safe!'

'This is not the King,' Sapt said. 'This is Rassendyll. The Six have taken the King away. We must find him.'

'Is the King in Zenda Castle?' asked Fritz. 'Is he alive?'

'Is the King in Zenda Castle? I don't know,' Sapt answered. 'Is he is alive? Yes! The Six will not kill the King today. They will wait for Black Michael. But Black Michael will get a message from the Six today. Then he will learn the truth about Rassendyll.'

I did not want to hear about Black Michael. I was tired. I got into the king's bed. I fell asleep quickly.

—

I woke at eleven o'clock. Later, I met some ministers of the Ruritanian government. Colonel Sapt talked to them. I did not speak.

In the afternoon, Colonel Sapt and I were talking in the king's sitting-room. Princess Flavia came into the room.

'Are you well, Your Majesty?' she asked me.

'I am very well,' I said.

She looked at me carefully. She looked at my eyes and my face. She smiled at me.

'You are a good man, Rudolf,' she said. 'And you will be a good king.'

'Yes, cousin,' I replied. 'Yes, I will be a good king. But a good king must have a wife. And a country must have a queen. Will you be my queen, Flavia? Will you marry me?'

Princess Flavia looked at the floor. She did not

answer my question. 'Your Majesty, you are very kind,' she said. 'I must go now.'

She walked towards the door. She did not look at me.

'Will you come to the palace tomorrow?' I asked.

The Princess turned round for a moment.

'Yes, I will come,' she said. Then she left the room.

'Very good, Mr Rassendyll,' said Colonel Sapt. 'You are an excellent actor.'

I did not answer him. I was not an actor. And I was not the real king. But I loved Princess Flavia!

A few minutes later, Fritz Tarlenheim came into the room. He was holding an envelope.

'A woman was waiting outside the palace,' he said to me. 'She brought this letter for you. She knows your real name.'

On the envelope was the name, 'Mr Rudolf Rassendyll'. I read the letter quickly.

Mr Rassendyll

Please do not show this letter to anybody. I know the truth about the coronation. I must talk to you.

Come to the summer-house in the palace garden. Come at midnight. Come alone. I will tell you everything then. I will answer all your questions.

There is danger for the King. Please come.

A

I showed the letter to Colonel Sapt.

'Who wrote this letter?' said the colonel. 'There will be a trap. You must not go to the summer-house.'

'I *must* go there!' I said. 'We want news of the King.'

'Yes. You are right,' said Sapt. 'You must go to the summer-house. But I will go with you.'

'Tell me about the summer-house, Colonel,' I said.

'It is a small wooden building at the end of the palace garden,' Sapt said. 'In hot weather, the royal family of Ruritania sits in the summer-house.'

———

At midnight, the colonel and I walked to the summer-house. There were some trees near the little building.

Sapt took a gun from his pocket.

'Take this gun,' he said quietly. 'I have a gun too. I will wait in the trees. Be very careful, Mr Rassendyll.'

I went to the door of the summer-house. A lamp was burning inside the building. I heard a woman's voice.

'Come in, Mr Rassendyll,' the woman said.

I opened the door. Inside the summer-house, I saw a small metal table and two chairs. And I saw a woman standing in a corner.

The woman was wearing a dark cloak. A dark scarf covered her face.

'Who are you?' I asked.

The woman uncovered her face. I knew her. She was Antoinette de Mauban. I closed the door behind me. There was a key in the lock of the door. I turned the key.

'Madame de Mauban,' I said. 'Did you write a letter to me? Will you answer my questions?'

'I did not write that letter,' said Madame de Mauban. 'The Duke of Strelsau wrote it.'

'And what does Black Michael want?' I asked.

'He wants to kill you!' she replied. 'This is a trap. The Duke's men will come here soon. You must leave the palace quickly. And you must leave Ruritania tonight!'

'Where is the King, Madame?' I asked.

'He is in Zenda Castle. He is a prisoner,' said Madame de Mauban. 'Three of Duke Michael's men are guarding him. They stay with him day and night. They never leave him.'

'Black Michael has six friends, Madame,' I said. 'Where are the other three?'

'We are here, Mr Rassendyll!' said a man's voice. The voice came from the other side of the door.

'They are early!' Antoinette de Mauban said. She was frightened.

'I love Duke Michael, Mr Rassendyll,' she said. 'But I am frightened of his anger. I wanted to help you. I am sorry.'

I looked round the summer-house. There was no other door. I stood near the door.

'What do you want?' I shouted.

'Come outside, Mr Rassendyll,' a man answered. 'We want to talk to you.'

'Talk to me now,' I said. 'Speak through the door. What do you want to say?'

'We will give you money,' said the man. 'We will give you fifty thousand English pounds. But you must leave the country tonight. And you must never return.'

'Don't go outside,' said Madame de Mauban quietly.

'I must help the King,' I said to her.

Quietly, I unlocked the door. Then I looked at the metal table. I picked it up. The table was heavy, but I could lift it.

'Come in!' I shouted. 'We will talk about the money.'

I held the table in front of me. Suddenly, the door opened. I heard three gun shots. Three men had fired bullets at me. But the bullets hit the metal table. The men started to come into the summer-house. I ran at them. I hit the three men with the table.

I jumped over the three men and I ran quickly into the garden. Colonel Sapt came running towards me.

I heard some more shots. Sapt fired his gun towards the summer-house.

'Go back to the palace!' Sapt shouted. 'Quickly!'

We ran towards the lights of the palace. There were many soldiers in the garden. The three men did not follow us. We were safe!

'It *was* a trap,' said Sapt. 'They tried to kill you.'

'But we have some information,' I said. 'The King is in Zenda Castle. You must go to Zenda. And you must go tomorrow!'

8

The Prisoner in the Castle

The next morning, Colonel Sapt woke me.

'Good morning, Mr Rassendyll,' he said. 'Black Michael has left the city. He has gone to Zenda Castle with three of his friends.'

'We must go to Zenda today, Colonel,' I said. 'The King is a prisoner in Zenda Castle. Black Michael will kill him soon! We must find King Rudolph and we must rescue him. Black Michael will be surprised!'

'Yes!' said Sapt. 'Black Michael will be surprised. And Black Michael will kill you! You mustn't come to Zenda Castle, Mr Rassendyll.'

'I will help my cousin, the King,' I said.

Colonel Sapt smiled.

'You are a good man, Mr Rassendyll,' he said. 'I will not stop you. I will speak to the Royal Guards. They hate Black Michael! They will come with us.'

———

In the afternoon, Princess Flavia came to the palace again. I was alone in the king's sitting-room. Flavia came into the room.

'Flavia, I am going to hunt in Zenda Forest,' I told her. 'I will leave Strelsau this afternoon.'

'I want to come with you, Rudolf,' said Princess Flavia.

'No, you must not come,' I replied. 'I am going to

hunt a very dangerous animal.'

'You are going to hunt Black Michael!' said the Princess.

'Yes,' I replied. 'Black Michael is bad for Ruritania!'

'Please be careful, Rudolf,' said the Princess. 'I will worry about you. I will not sleep. I am frightened of Black Michael.'

I held Flavia's hand for a moment. 'Be careful,' she said again. Then she quickly left the room.

A moment later, Sapt and Fritz came into the room.

'The Royal Guards will come with us to Zenda,' Sapt said. 'Fritz has a large house in Zenda Forest. We will stay there.'

———

Late in the afternoon, we left Strelsau. We travelled by train. We got off the train at the small station near Zenda Forest. Horses were waiting for us at the station. We rode into the forest. Soon, we arrived at Fritz's house.

'You and I will eat at the inn in Zenda tonight,' I told Fritz. 'I will talk to the innkeeper's daughter. I have a plan.'

At nine o'clock, Fritz and I rode to the inn.

'I will cover my face with a scarf,' I said to him.

'And I will cover my red hair with a hat. Nobody will know me. Fritz, you must go into the inn first. Ask for a private dining-room. And ask for some food and a bottle of wine.'

'Yes, I'll do those things,' said Fritz. 'But why?'

'The innkeeper's daughter will bring the food and the wine.' I said. 'She has a friend called Johann. Johann is one of Black Michael's servants. Johann works at Zenda Castle. We must speak to him. We must ask for his help. The girl will send a message to him.'

'But the girl has seen you before,' said Fritz. 'Will she help you?'

'She has seen Mr Rassendyll from England,' I replied. 'But he had a beard. This evening, she will look at me and she will see the King of Ruritania!'

We arrived at the inn, and Fritz went in first. After a minute, he called to me. I went into the inn. Nobody saw my face. Fritz took me to a private dining-room. Soon, the innkeeper's daughter came into the room with a bottle of wine.

I was wearing my scarf and hat. I spoke to the girl.

'Have you seen a newspaper?' I asked her. 'Have you seen pictures of the King's coronation?'

'Yes, I have seen the pictures, sir,' she said. 'The King is a good-looking man.'

I took off my scarf and hat. I uncovered my face.

'Do you know me?' I asked.

The girl dropped the wine bottle on the floor.

'You are the King, sir!' she said.

'Don't be frightened,' I said. 'But don't tell anybody about my visit. This visit is a secret.'

'I won't tell anybody, Your Majesty,' said the innkeeper's daughter.

'Do you know the servants at Zenda Castle?' I asked the girl. 'Do you have friend in the castle?'

'Yes, Your Majesty,' said the young girl. 'My friend, Johann, works at the castle. He is one of Duke Michael's servants.'

'We want to talk to Johann,' I said. 'Will he come here tomorrow night?'

'I will send a message to him, Your Majesty,' said the girl. 'He will come.'

'Good,' I said. 'But remember my words. My visit is a secret. Don't tell Johann about my visit. Don't tell *anybody* about my visit!'

9

Rupert Hentzau

The next morning, one of Duke Michael's friends visited me at Fritz's house. He was one of the Six. He was a young, very good-looking man. He rode up to the house at ten o'clock and he spoke to one of the guards.

'I want to see the King,' he told the soldier.

I went to the front door of the house.

'Who are you?' I asked the young man. 'And what do you want?'

'My name is Rupert Hentzau,' the young man said. 'I want to speak to you alone. I have a message from the Duke of Strelsau.' He was not a polite young man.

I spoke to the guard.

'Do not follow us,' I told him. Then I walked away from the house. Rupert Hentzau walked beside me.

'Good!' said Rupert Hentzau, 'Now we are alone, Mr Rassendyll.'

'You must call me "Your Majesty",' I said.

'That is a bad joke!' said Rupert Hentzau.

'What is Duke Michael's message?' I asked.

'You must leave Ruritania,' said the young man. 'The Duke will give you one hundred thousand pounds. The border is twelve kilometres from here. The Duke will give you the money at the border. But you must never come back to Ruritania. And you must leave the country today.'

'No, I will not leave Ruritania,' I said.

'I am not surprised by your answer,' said Hentzau. 'I told Duke Michael, "Rassendyll will not take your money." I was right.'

'Is the King alive and well?' I asked.

'The King is alive,' said Rupert Hentzau. 'And is Princess Flavia well?'

'She is well,' I answered.

'I will give that news to the Duke,' said Rupert Hentzau. 'He will be happy! He will soon be the king. And Princess Flavia will soon get married. She will marry King Michael.'

'No! She will never marry Black Michael!' I said angrily.

Rupert Hentzau looked at me carefully. He laughed.

'Ah, I understand,' he said. 'You love the Princess. And does the Princess love you?'

I did not reply. I looked at the ground.

'Listen to me, Rassendyll! I will help you,' said Hentzau. 'Leave the country today. Take Princess Flavia with you. I will not tell the Duke. He will know tomorrow. But tomorrow, you will be far away.'

'I will kill Rudolf today,' Hentzau said. 'Tomorrow, Michael will be the king. You will have the Princess. Both of you will be happy!'

For a moment, I did not answer him. For a moment I thought about his words. I did not want Black Michael's money. But I loved Princess Flavia.

Then I was very angry. I was angry with Hentzau. And I was angry with myself!

'Get onto your horse and go!' I said to Rupert Hentzau. 'Do not speak to me again!'

Rupert Hentzau laughed and he walked towards his horse. I walked beside him. I wanted him to leave immediately. Then suddenly, he turned towards me. There was a knife in his hand. He was going to kill me! I put up my left hand and I pushed his arm away. The knife cut my shoulder. I shouted to the soldiers.

The guards ran towards me. Rupert got on his horse and he quickly rode away. He was laughing.

———

That evening, some of the guards waited near the inn in Zenda. They waited for Johann. Johann was going to visit the innkeeper's daughter. The soldiers saw Johann coming. They put a coat over his head and they brought him to Fritz's house.

Johann was very frightened. Colonel Sapt told Johann the truth about the coronation.

'You have met Mr Rassendyll before,' Sapt said.

Then I asked Johann some questions.

'Where is the King?' I asked.

'He is in the castle. He is in a cell,' Johann replied. 'He is a prisoner. There are three guards. Two guards are always in a room outside the cell. The other guard is always in the cell, with the King.'

'We must bring the King out of the castle,' I said. 'We must rescue him. Duke Michael wants to kill him.'

'That will be difficult,' said Johann. 'All the guards have guns and swords. The guards will see you coming. They will kill the King.'

'We will try to kill them,' I said. 'Will you help us?'

'Yes, sir, I will help you,' answered Johann. 'Another person will help you too.'

'Who is this other person?' I asked.

'Madame de Mauban,' answered Johann. 'She is a

prisoner in the castle.'

'Why is she a prisoner?' I asked.

'She wants to leave Ruritania,' Johann replied. 'She is frightened of Duke Michael. She wants to go back to France. But the Duke will not let her go.'

'I want to get into the castle tomorrow night,' I told Johann. 'But the gate will be closed. And the servants pull up the drawbridge at night. Am I right?'

'Yes, sir,' said Johann.

'Is there another entrance to the castle?' I asked.

'Yes. There is a small door,' said Johann. 'It is ten metres from the drawbridge, on the left. You can get to it in a boat. But all the boats are inside the castle.'

'Johann,' I said. 'Will you open that small door for me tomorrow, at midnight?'

'Yes, sir,' said Johann. 'I want to help the King.'

'Good! You will open the door for me,' I said. 'Then we will put down the drawbridge and we will open the gate. My friends will bring the soldiers over the drawbridge. We will rescue the King.'

'How will you kill the King's guards, sir?' Johann asked.

'I have a plan,' I said. 'I must write a letter.'

'I must go back to the castle now, sir,' said Johann. 'The gate will be closed soon. And soon, the servants will pull up the drawbridge.'

I quickly wrote a letter. The letter was for Madame de Mauban. I gave the letter to Johann. He ran back to the castle.

10

Voices from a Window

The next day was Sunday. We rested at Fritz Tarlenheim's house all day. Then at eleven o'clock, Fritz, Sapt and I said good luck to each other.

Sapt and Fritz were going to wait in the forest near the castle.

'Johann and I will put down the drawbridge,' I told them. 'We will open the gate. Then you must ride into the castle with the Royal Guards. You must come quickly. Black Michael's guards will fight us. It will be very dangerous! But no other plan is possible. We must rescue the King tonight.'

Fritz, Sapt and the soldiers went into the forest with their horses. I went to Zenda Castle alone. I was wearing dark clothes. I took a knife with me but I did not take a gun.

I walked quietly through Zenda Forest. The tall pine trees were all around me. The trees had a strong smell. There was some light from the moon.

Soon, I came to the moat of the castle. I was two hundred metres from the drawbridge. There were guards near the castle gate, but they could not see me.

I swam across the moat.

There was a ledge between the castle and the moat. The ledge was a narrow path. I pulled myself out of the moat and I stood on the ledge. I walked slowly along the ledge towards the drawbridge.

There were guards on top of the castle walls. I could hear them, but I could not see them. And they could not see me.

Suddenly, a window opened. It was two metres above my head. I stopped walking. Somebody was standing near the window.

I heard two voices. A man and a woman were talking.

'Antoinette, forget about Michael. I love you,' said the man. It was the voice of Rupert Hentzau.

Then I heard Madame de Mauban's voice.

'Leave this room!' she said. 'I hate you! Michael will come here soon. He will be angry with you.'

'Michael does not love you,' said Rupert Hentzau. 'He wants to be the King. He wants to marry Flavia.'

Then I heard a third voice. It was the voice of Black Michael.

'Why are you here, Rupert?' he said angrily.

'The lady was alone. I was talking to her,' said Rupert Hentzau.

'Leave us,' said Black Michael. 'It is late. Go to your room.'

'I am not tired,' said Rupert.

'Leave us!' Black Michael shouted. 'I want to speak to Madame de Mauban.'

'I will talk to you again, Madame,' said Rupert Hentzau.

A door closed loudly. Then the window closed too.

11
Inside the Castle

I walked along the ledge again. I was looking for a small door in the wall of the castle. Soon, I found it. I heard the bell of the castle clock. It was midnight!

The small door opened quietly. Johann was standing inside the door. He took me into the castle. He took me to some stone stairs. He pointed down the stairs.

'The King's cell is down there,' said the big man. 'There are two guards in a room outside the cell. They are two of the Duke's friends – two of the Six. Their names are De Gautet and Bersonin. They are bad men!'

'The door of the cell is locked,' Johann said. 'And another man is in the cell with the King. That man is called Detchard. There is a doctor in the cell too.'

'Is the King ill?' I asked.

'Yes,' replied Johann. 'He is sick. The doctor is going to stay with him tonight.'

'Where is the key of the cell?' I asked.

'The key is on a table, outside the cell,' said Johann.

'Did you give my letter to Madame de Mauban?' I asked.

'Yes, sir,' he replied.

'Good! She will help us,' I said. 'I told her about my plan in the letter. Soon, she will start to shout. The guards will run to her room. Then we must open the castle gate. And we must put down the drawbridge. Our soldiers are waiting in the forest.'

'I will open the gate and I will put down the drawbridge, sir,' said Johann. 'You must go to the King's cell. You must kill the guards!'

Johann went towards the castle gate. I walked down the stairs. I walked quietly along a corridor. My knife was in my hand. Then I saw a light. The light was coming from a room on the left. And I heard voices. Two men were talking.

At that moment I heard a shout. The shout came from somewhere above me.

'Help! Michael, help! Hentzau is in my room. Help me!'

It was the voice of Antoinette de Mauban.

A man came out of the room on my left. He had a sword. 'What is happening?' he shouted.

I knocked the man to the floor. Then I pushed my knife into his chest. In a moment, he was dead!

The other man shouted from the room. 'Who is there, De Gautet?' he shouted.

I took the dead man's sword and I ran into the room. On the left, was the door of the King's cell. On the right, was the other man – Bersonin.

Bersonin shouted to his friend inside the cell.

'Kill the King, Detchard!' he shouted.

Then he started to fight me. But Bersonin was not a good fighter. Quickly, I killed him with the sword.

Where was the key of the cell door? I saw it on a

small table. In a moment, I had opened the door. I was inside the cell!

The King was lying on a bed in a corner. He was tired and sick. I saw the doctor sitting on a chair near the bed. He was shouting at another man – Detchard.

'No! No! Stop!' the doctor shouted.

Detchard had a sword in his hand. He was walking towards the King. Suddenly, he ran to the doctor and knocked him off the chair. Then he killed the doctor with his sword.

Detchard started walking towards the King again. He was going to kill him. But then Detchard heard me behind him. He turned towards me.

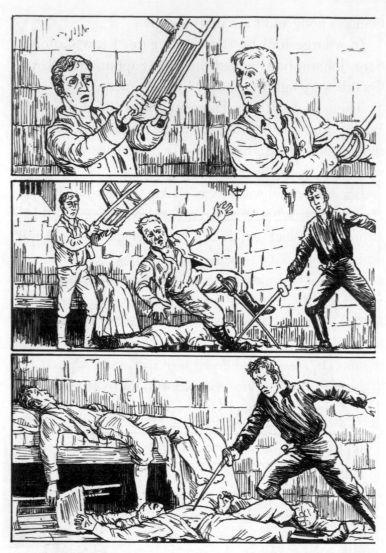

I had killed Detchard. I ran to the King. King
Rudolf was ill and tired. But he was alive!

I ran out of the cell and I ran through the next
room. I ran into the corridor. I jumped over De

Gautet's body and I ran up the stairs.

In a large hall by the castle gate, I saw Colonel Sapt. Johann had opened the gate. Sapt and the Royal Guards were fighting Duke Michael's men.

Then I saw Rupert Hentzau. He was fighting too. But he was not fighting Colonel Sapt's men. He was fighting Black Michael. The two men were fighting with their swords.

Black Michael was a very strong fighter. But Rupert Hentzau was a better fighter. Suddenly, he pushed his sword into Black Michael's body. Black Michael fell down. He started to speak. But then he died.

Three of Colonel Sapt's soldiers ran towards Rupert Hentzau. But Hentzau ran up some stairs. I followed him quickly. Hentzau ran along a corridor. He ran to a high window. He opened the window and he jumped through it. He jumped down into the moat.

I ran to the window and I looked down at the moat. The moon was bright. I saw Rupert  Hentzau swimming across the moat.

'Stop, Hentzau! Stop!' I shouted.

Rupert Hentzau swam to the other side of the moat. He pulled himself out of the water. He looked up at me.

'We will meet again, Rassendyll!' he shouted. Then he ran into the forest.

A few moments later, Fritz Tarlenheim came up the stairs and he walked towards me.

'Hentzau has gone,' I said.

'The King is alive,' I told Fritz. 'He is tired and ill, but he is alive. You must send the news to Princess Flavia.'

Fritz looked at me carefully.

'Princess Flavia is here,' he said. 'She was worried. She came to Zenda tonight. She wanted to see —. She wanted to see the King. *You* must tell her the news, Mr Rassendyll.'

'No, no!' I said. 'The Princess must not see me. Take her to the King. Take her to King Rudolf. She must marry him. I must go away now!'

But at that moment, Princess Flavia came towards us. She looked at my face.

'Rudolf?' she said. 'Are you Rudolf?'

'No,' I said. 'I am not the King.'

'This is Mr Rudolf Rassendyll, from England,' said Fritz. 'He is our friend.'

'But your face —,' said Princess Flavia.

'The King is safe,' I said quietly. 'He is waiting for you.'

'Ah – there are two Rudolfs,' said Princess Flavia sadly. 'I understand now. You helped the King. You helped me. I will always remember you, Rudolf.'

'And I will always remember you, Flavia,' I said.

We looked at each other. We loved each other. But I had to go, and she had to marry the King.

The Princess turned and she walked away. But she looked back at me.

12
The End of My Story

At last, we left Zenda Castle. Fritz Tarlenheim took me to his house in Zenda Forest. I stayed there for a day. Fritz gave me some clothes and some money.

Early the next morning, I walked across the border. Soon, I was in Dresden. From Dresden, I travelled to Paris. I stayed in Paris for a week.

Madame de Mauban arrived in Paris too. I did not meet her, but I saw her name in the newspapers. She was going to live at her house outside Paris.

After a week, I travelled to London. There, I read about the marriage of the Princess Flavia and King Rudolf the Fifth of Ruritania. I smiled. But I was sad.

It is 1898. I am thirty-four years old now and I am not married. I will never get married. In August every year, I travel to Dresden. I stay there for one week, and I meet my friend Fritz Tarlenheim. Every year, Fritz gives me a letter and a flower – a white rose. The letter and the flower come from a lady with wonderful red hair.

I enjoy my week in Dresden every August. But I live in London. I often meet my brother. But I do not go to his house. My sister-in-law is angry with me. Why is Rose angry with me? I did not get a job. I did not become a diplomat. But I *did* write a book – *The Prisoner of Zenda*.

Published by Macmillan Heinemann ELT
Between Towns Road, Oxford OX4 3PP
Macmillan Heinemann ELT is an imprint of
Macmillan Publishers Limited
Companies and representatives throughout the world

ISBN 0 435 27340 X

These retold versions by Stephen Colburn for Macmillan Guided Readers

Text © John Hope-Hawkins 1998, 2002
First published 1998

Design and illustration © Macmillan Publishers Limited 1998, 2002
Heinemann is a registered trademark of Reed Educational & Professional Publishing Limited
This version first published 2002

Acknowledgements: The publishers would like to thank Popperforo for
permission to reproduce the picture on page 4.

Illustrated by Kay Dixey
Map on page 3 and illustrations on page 5 by John Gilkes
Cover by Stewart Rees and Marketplace Design

Printed in China

2006 2005 2004 2003 2002
13 12 11 10 9 8 7 6 5 4